WITHDRAWN

For Buda. Your big heart inspires me every day.
— T.G. (Auntie)

To my best friend Nazaria, who has always been
a giant from the inside out.
— S.C.

First published in 2023 by Page Street Kids
an imprint of
Page Street Publishing Co.
27 Congress Street, Suite 1511
Salem, MA 01970
www.pagestreetpublishing.com

Distributed by Macmillan, sales in Canada by The Canadian Manda Group

22 23 24 25 26 CCO 5 4 3 2 1
ISBN-13: 978-1-64567-630-0
ISBN-10: 1-64567-630-7

CIP data for this book is available from the Library of Congress.

This book was typeset in Instant Harmony.
The illustrations were done digitally.
Cover and book design by Melia Parsloe for Page Street Kids.
Edited by Kayla Tostevin for Page Street Kids.

Printed and bound in Shenzhen, Guangdong, China

Page Street Publishing uses only materials from suppliers who are committed to responsible
and sustainable forest management.

Page Street Publishing protects our planet by donating to nonprofits like The Trustees,
which focuses on local land conservation.

I WANT TO BE BIG!

Tiffany Golden

illustrated by **Sawyer Cloud**

PAGE
STREET
KIDS

I want to be big.
Bigger than Big Brother.
Bigger than Big Sister.
Bigger than Mom.
Bigger than Dad.

Bigger than everyone!
BIG!

When you're big you can . . .
Mess up your room.
Eat all the candy.

Stay up really late.
Reach the tallest counter!

You can . . .

Swim with sharks.

Be best friends with Bigfoot.

Dig to the center of the Earth.

Go to the moon!

Nobody's your boss when you're big.

Hmph!

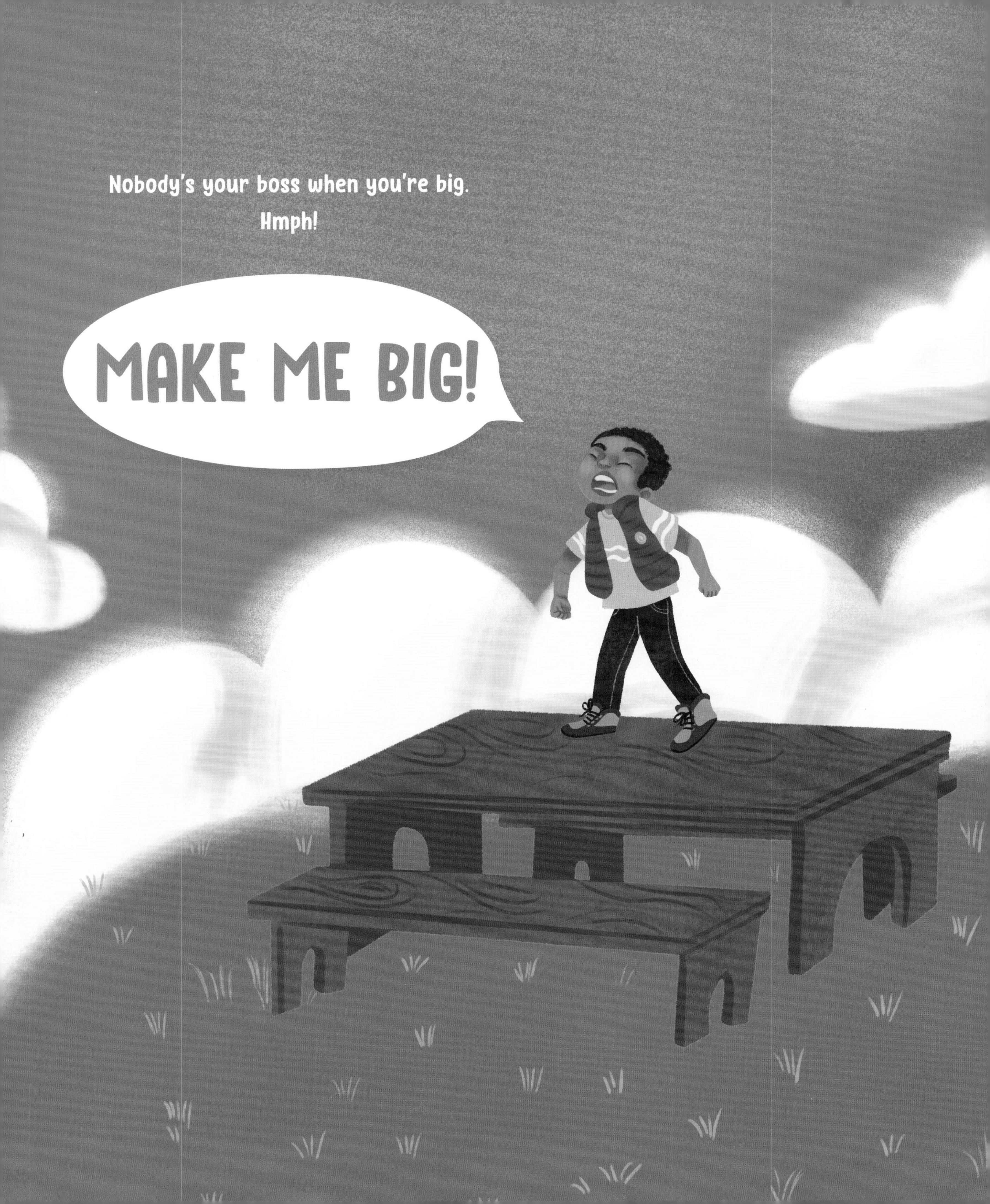

Whoa . . . .

I *am* big.

Bigger than Big Brother.
Bigger than Big Sister.
Bigger than Mom.
Bigger than Dad.

Bigger than everyone!

BIG!

Nobody's my boss! YAY!
I can drive really big cars,
and jet ski the ocean,

skateboard on rainbows,
or jump *really* far!

Being big is SO much fun!
I bet being bigger will be even better!

Bigger than bears.
Bigger than trees.
Bigger than buildings.
Bigger than everything!

Make me **BIGGER!**

Um, uh-oh.

I am *big* big.

Bigger than a whale.
Bigger than a redwood.
Bigger than a mountain.
Bigger than everything!

Oh no! Bigger is *too* big.

Too big to tame lions.
Too big to wrestle bears.
Too big to windsurf with seals.
Too big for everything.

Too big
to glide down the slide,
or get piggyback rides,
or wear my favorite red pants,
and march with the ants!

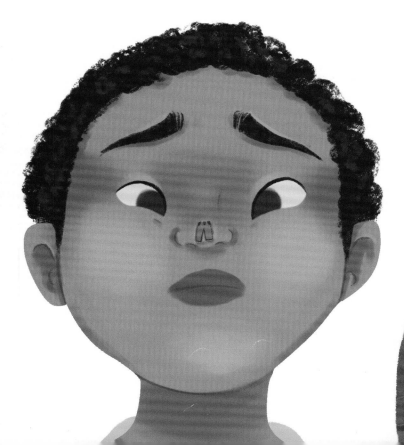

Too big
to jump in puddles with Big Brother,
or find terrific treasures with Big Sister,
or sit on Mom's cozy lap
or Dad's strong shoulders.
Too big for everything that I love.

This is *not* how I thought big would be!
I just want to make my own sandwich,
and get my own cookies . . .

Do things myself and not wait for someone big!
Hmph!

Hey! I may be small.

Smaller than Big Brother.
Smaller than Big Sister.
Smaller than Mom.
Smaller than Dad.
Smaller than everyone!

But with a little help, I can do anything.